A true story

UNFOLD 21

"The Journey That Made Me"

KEVIN

INKTHOUGHT
PRESS

INKTHOUGHT
PRESS

Made with ♥ INKTHOUGHT PRESS

ACKNOLEDGEMENT

As I look back on this incredible journey, my heart is overflowing with gratitude. This book would not have been possible without the love, guidance, and support of so many wonderful people who have touched my life in ways words can scarcely express.

First and foremost, I offer my deepest thanks to the Almighty God—my constant strength, my guiding light, and the source of every blessing. Without His grace, none of this would have been possible.

To my family, for your unconditional love, patience, and encouragement—you have been my anchor in every storm and my cheer in every triumph.

To my friends Amarnath, Babu, Benita Albert, Blessy, Jonathan, Kavithran, Krishna, Thriksha, Sarnaya, and Vignesh. Thank you for filling my life with laughter, light, and unforgettable memories. Your friendship has been a haven, a source of motivation, and a wellspring of joy throughout this chapter of my life.

To my colleagues and mentors—Aishwarya, Alex, Annie, Anu, Beena, Benita, Blessy, Caroline, Dhiya, Esther, Hannah, Jayapriya, Jeevitha, Joanna, Kavitha, Keerthika, Mary Pramila, Mary Uma, Meena, Meenu, Mercy, Monica, Nandini M, Nandhini, Nathaniel, Pavithra, Preetha, Preethi, Premila, Priyanka, Rachel, Rashmi, Rhema, Samuel, Sekar, Shanmugam, Sharon Grace, Srinivas,

Suniliga, Thivya, and Vijaya—thank you for sharing your wisdom, guiding me in moments of doubt, and reminding me that learning never ends.

A special note of gratitude to my professors. Ms.Prasitha, Mr. Kumaran, and Mr. Udhay. Thank you for believing in me, for your patience in guiding me, and for shaping my thoughts and skills through your dedication and insight.

To each person who gave me their time, shared their happiness, and became a part of my story, thank you for making this year truly unforgettable. The experiences we shared, the lessons we learned together, and the bonds we built will always hold a special place in my heart.

This book is as much yours as it is mine.

PROLOGUE

They say life moves in a straight line, but mine has taken countless turns. At every unexpected fork, I stood with trembling hands, choosing between dream and duty, hope and hesitation. I wasn't born into certainty. I come from a small town where dreams are often whispered, not shouted, where success is measured in degrees and stable jobs, not in stories like this. I once imagined a simple path: study hard, make my family proud, maybe one day see my name on a hospital door. But life, as it turns out, had a different script. This journey hasn't been smooth or simple.

There were nights filled with restless questions, moments of failure I never saw coming, and quiet decisions that changed everything. I've battled doubt, drifted through confusion, and clung to faith when nothing else made sense. Yet, during all that chaos, something unexpected happened: a transformation. And it didn't happen in a grand auditorium or a moment of applause. It happened in hospital corridors, in the eyes of children who couldn't speak, and in the gentle lessons taught by silence.

What began as just a year of work in Vellore became the most defining chapter of my life. It's here, through therapy sessions and tearful goodbyes, late-night reflections and small wins, that I found pieces of myself I didn't know were missing. If you've ever felt lost in the middle of your own story or wondered if purpose can be found in the waiting, this book is for you. Walk with me through the mess, the magic, and the meaning. This is more than a memoir; it's a mirror. And maybe, just maybe, it's the beginning of something new.
Because the most extraordinary chapters often begin right where certainty ends.

CONTENTS

Part 1
BEFORE IT ALL BEGAN

Every story has a quiet time before it starts, a moment when dreams are just beginning and the future feels wide open. This is the time before big changes, before new steps and new journeys.

Here, in the place where I grew up, life was full of small joys and simple moments. The sun shone through the windows, laughter filled the air, and I dreamed of what might come next.

Before anything begins, there is hope, questions, and a little nervousness - wondering if I'm ready for what's ahead.

Part 1 is about this peaceful time before everything starts—a time to remember where I came from and get ready for what's to come. It is the start of my story and the beginning of who I will become.

"Before the path appears, there is wonder and endless possibility."

1
Who is this?

I am Kevin, a simple guy who grew up in a small town at the southern tip of India. Raised in a close-knit family, I found security in routines, warmth in family gatherings, and strength in the modest dreams of my childhood. My world was familiar and reassuring, but I also carried big dreams within my heart.

When I turned 18, my life leaped as I moved to Chennai, the city known as "Vandharai Vazhavaikkum Chennai," a place that welcomes and elevates everyone who comes with hope. Leaving home for my undergraduate studies meant stepping into a new world of endless possibilities. I joined one of the city's most famous colleges, my heart brimming with ambition and the curiosity of youth.

It was during these years that I first became aware of the field of Speech-Language Pathology (SLP). What started as curiosity soon became fascination as I discovered how this profession transforms lives by helping people communicate effectively. From simply knowing about SLP, I found myself drawn towards the science and service it represents, slowly transitioning from knowing SLP to aspiring and working towards being an SLP. Today, I am pursuing my studies to become an Audiologist and Speech-Language Pathologist, eager to make a difference in this field.

As the years quickly passed and I approached the end of my college days, I often thought about how people saw me. Many who didn't know me said I was rude, full of attitude, or even a scoundrel. But those truly close to me, my limited but genuine friends, and my loving partner with whom I shared a beautiful love story, understood a different side. They knew the loyal, caring, and sometimes quietly vulnerable side that rarely showed in public.

During my final year, life was full of uncertainty. Like many students, I stood at a crossroads:

- Should I continue my studies?
- Should I start working?
- Was I ready for the next big step?

I sought advice from seniors and professors, listened to their stories, and tried to imagine myself in different futures. But behind every conversation and suggestion, a bigger question kept echoing inside:

"What am I going to do?"
This stage of my life was marked by restlessness, hope, and searching—a time when the answers weren't clear, but the journey itself began shaping who I was becoming.

2

The Call

One rainy night, everything changed with a single phone call. I was alone in my sister's apartment on the 10th floor, watching the city lights flicker through thick, rain-filled clouds. It was quiet except for the soft hum of the elevator. Around nine o'clock, my phone rang. It was a good friend from my internship, someone younger who always called me "Anna, Anna" — brother, brother with respect and warmth.

His voice was excited, almost urgent:
"Anna, there's a vacancy in CMC! You should apply right now!"

I didn't know what to do or how to apply, but he patiently sent me a link and helped me step by step. That's when I realized it was the last day to apply. Suddenly, I was in a race against time! They wanted certificates and letters from three people, which I didn't have.

My heart was pounding as I quickly filled out the basic details, hoping it would work. After submitting the form in such a hurry, I felt sure my chance was over. I didn't expect ever to hear back.

I went back to finishing my internship, trying not to think about the application. Days went by. I nearly forgot about the job.

Then, one evening at home, my phone rang again. I picked up.
“Hello, is this Kevin?”
“Yes, ma’am?”
“This is CMC. Are you coming for the interview?”

My heart skipped a beat. “Yes, ma’am,” I replied, trying to sound brave. I was shocked and a little scared, but I knew I had to go. I packed quickly and took a bus from Nagercoil to Vellore, my head full of dreams, what if I got the job? What would my life be like? I fell asleep on the bus with these questions swirling in my mind.

When the bus reached Vellore early in the morning, the conductor called out, “Vellore, Vellore!” My friend, my “Anna,” was there to pick me up. I went to my aunt's house, freshened up, and started reading my notes, getting ready for the big day. My aunt made me hot sambar with pongal; it was delicious, comforting, just what I needed before such an important moment.

My uncle then took me to the famous, 125-year-old Christian Medical College. It was my first time seeing the place. The campus was busy, full of people everywhere. Our car passed through the main gate and stopped in front of the ISSCC building. My uncle smiled and said, “All the best, Kevin.” With those words, I took my first real step into CMC.

The security guard at the entrance asked, “Where are you going?”
“I’m here for an interview in 550 Developmental Pediatrics, first floor,” I replied, trying to sound confident.

And so began a new chapter, started with just a phone call and a little bit of courage.

3
The Interview Day

I walked through the halls, searching for room 550. When I reached the reception, a bold, fearless lady sat behind the desk. "I came for the interview," I told her. She looked straight at me and said loudly, "Wait there." I nodded and sat down.

A little later, another kind woman approached me. She explained, "We're waiting for a few more people. Then we will start." I realized I had arrived too early because of my nerves. Time ticked by. No one else showed up, and soon I was alone in a quiet room filled with empty chairs. That made me even more anxious.

Then, a quiet lady came in and announced, "You'll have a written exam first, followed by a practical, and then the interview." She handed me the question paper. Relief washed over me. I knew the answers and wrote confidently. Next was the practical tcst, which I also handled well.

Finally, it was time for the scariest part: the interview. My name echoed down the hallway, “Kevin, Kevin!” The door opened, I stepped through, and it shut behind me. My heart was racing, but I knew this was my moment.

The moment I stepped into the interview room, my nerves kicked in. Across the table sat three legendary doctors, two of them renowned pioneers in developmental pediatrics. It felt like I was surrounded, no way to hide my anxious heart.

They began with a quick boost: “You did well in the written and practical tests.” Their words instantly made me more confident. Then one of them asked, “What is your field of expertise?”

Taking a deep breath, I answered, “I like working with children who have motor speech disorders and adults with language disorders.”

They asked me a few technical questions. I answered about half of them, feeling the pressure build. The lady doctor sitting closest to me looked especially bold and fearless. She asked, “Can you tell us the DSM-5 criteria for autism?”

My mind went blank. “Two out of five,” I replied, which was not the answer she wanted. Her disappointment was clear, and I felt fear wash over me. This was my very first interview, and now I was sweating with anxiety.

Thankfully, another doctor shifted the conversation.
“What do you like to do?” he asked warmly.
“I like to play football,” I smiled, trying to relax.
“Do you play guitar?” he continued.

"No, I'm not very good at music," I admitted. He laughed, lightening the mood, and told me there were football turfs I could play on. Then he asked about my family and some basic details.

Soon, the interview was over. "Kevin, wait outside," they said. I left the room, trying to calm my racing heart. A few minutes later, the doctor stepped out and asked, "When can you join?"

"I'll join after finishing my internship," I replied. "Okay," he nodded.

My heart soared with happiness. I wanted to jump up and down, and as I walked out of the hospital, I felt pure joy. This was the first big step towards a new chapter in my life.

UNFOLD 21

4

The long 12-hour journey

The day arrived; the day I would leave the comfort of my home and the familiar rhythms of Nagercoil behind. The morning was filled with quiet goodbyes and lingering hugs. My family, always my shelter and strength, tried to hide their emotions, but in every glance, I could see pride mixed with worry.

As I packed the last bag, memories swirled: the aromas drifting from my mother's kitchen, the afternoon laughter with my siblings, and the peaceful pace of our small town. Each room seemed to whisper childhood stories, and with every step toward the door, leaving became a little harder.

The bus to Vellore felt like a bridge between two worlds. The landscape shifted from the green fields around Nagercoil to sights I had only imagined. Through the window, I watched every mile glide by and wondered, with a mix of excitement and anxiety, what kind of person I would become away from everything I knew.

In those quiet hours, I reflected on what home truly meant: a place shaped by people and memories, not just walls and streets. I promised myself to carry that foundation with me, even as I stepped into something entirely unknown.

Arriving in Vellore, I was greeted not by the familiar calm of home, but by the city's constant motion, the buzz of traffic, the bright lights, the energy of people everywhere. I felt lost and alive at the same time. College in Vellore was a world apart: new faces, new rules, endless possibilities. Each challenge forced me to adapt, to solve problems on my own, and to gradually build real confidence.

Yet true growth came not just from learning independence. It came from meeting inspiring mentors, discovering my passion for Speech-Language Pathology, and building friendships that shaped my journey. There were moments of loneliness, but every setback revealed new sources of strength and hope within me.

Leaving home was hard, but it was also a powerful invitation to grow—to become the person I was meant to be. My story, far from ending with goodbye, was just beginning to unfold—one choice at a time—in the wide and welcoming world beyond my first home, here in Vellore.

PART 2
A NEW LIFE BEGINS

There comes a time when you leave the world you know and step into something new and unfamiliar. Living on your own for the first time means letting go of the voices and routines you grew up with, and learning what independence feels like.

These chapters are about new beginnings in small rooms, dreaming big, and sometimes feeling restless and alone. In these quiet moments, fears teach you important lessons and doubts help you find your hidden strengths.
Every day is uncertain, but every night you hold onto the hope that you are slowly becoming the person you want to be.

This section is about learning to adapt to new routines, trusting yourself, and finding happiness in small successes. It's about growing through real experiences that no book can truly teach you.

Whisper of hope:
"Maybe, just maybe, I'm becoming the person I wished to be."

5
Own sanctuary

On a bright and sunny morning, I set out to find a place I could finally call my own. After searching, I found a cozy little house—a 1BHK on the first floor, with two balconies overlooking a few gentle trees swaying nearby. It was simple, yet it held everything I needed to begin this new chapter of my life. Living alone as a bachelor was a journey full of new challenges and small victories.

I woke early each day, preparing simple breakfasts of eggs, oats, legumes, and fresh fruits. Cooking lunch was a rare treat, usually reserved for Sundays, while most evenings, I ate porridge or egg scramble with bread. Sometimes, when tiredness crept in, I would order food, knowing that managing a home was no small task.

Cleaning became a weekly ritual—mopping the floor and tidying up the space that was now truly mine. The bills for groceries, electricity, and water were my responsibility, and learning to budget and save taught me lessons that went far beyond numbers.

Though the house was rented, it felt like my own sanctuary. This small, simple home marked the beginning of a new journey—a quiet, steady path toward independence and self-reliance. Each day, I grew a little stronger, more confident, and more connected to the life I was building on my own.

6

First day at CMC

My First Day as a Junior Speech Therapist. My first day at Christian Medical College wasn't just wonderful—it was a day I'll never forget. Walking through the gates, I felt a mix of excitement and nerves. This place was more than a famous hospital; it was a world of history and hope, with sunlight shining through the trees and people moving with purpose everywhere I looked.

Inside, my heart beat quickly. The halls felt alive with stories of those who had come before me. I wasn't just entering a building—I was about to become part of something much bigger. Warm welcomes from my colleagues and senior faculty helped calm my nerves. During my orientation and department tour, I met many professionals: pediatric doctors, psychologists, occupational therapists, and more. Each person was busy but always smiling, reminding me I'd joined a true team.

But what made this first day truly memorable were the children. As a junior speech therapist, I started as an observer, assisting my seniors as they guided me through the day's sessions. There were six in total, each one different and challenging in its way.

What surprised me most was the languages. The first child spoke Telugu, and I could only smile and try my best to understand. The next was a child speaking Hindi, followed by others who spoke Malayalam, Bangla, then English, and finally, my native language, Tamil. For the first time, I realized just how many languages fill our world—and how little I knew beyond Tamil and English. At one point, I felt worried. How could I truly help each child without understanding their language?

I quickly learned my first real lesson as a speech therapist: "Language is incredibly important—and to help others, it's something I must keep learning."

Looking back, my first day wasn't about doing everything perfectly. It was about discovering the world's diversity and understanding that true care begins with listening and learning, especially from those very different from myself. Every challenge, every language, and every new face became the start of a journey to grow—not only as a professional but as a person.

7
Fear, Doubts, and First Success

My first few months as a junior speech therapist were filled with fear and self-doubt. The shift from classroom theory to working with real children was jarring—learning about language milestones in textbooks was one thing; facing a child and a concerned parent, quite another.

Each morning, I walked into the clinic wondering, *"Am I ready for this? What if I'm wrong? What if I say the wrong thing?"* My hands trembled during assessments, my eyes instinctively searched the room for help, and most days, I found myself looking up to my seniors, who made things look so effortless.

They read case files with ease, answered questions confidently, made instant decisions, managed anxious parents, and provided therapy with grace. I, meanwhile, struggled just to choose the right screening tool or find the right words to explain something gently.

After every session, I'd replay the entire appointment in my head—what I said, what I didn't say, what I should've said. It felt like a silent battle within, but I kept showing up. Little by little, my seniors began to notice. They guided me patiently, step by step. One of them told me, "It's normal to feel scared when you're just starting—keep learning, keep showing up."

Then came the turning point.

One afternoon, I was asked to handle a session alone. My heart pounded. A five-year-old boy had arrived with his parents, all the way from the *City of Joy*, Kolkata. The child was completely non-verbal. His parents carried years of worry on their faces and a bag full of paperwork from therapy centers across India. When they sat down, they asked me the question I had now heard many times:

"Will our child ever speak?"

I paused. Not just because it's a difficult question, but because I now understand that it's never just about speech. It's about being understood. It's about connection. I gently replied, "Speech is just one way of communication. But it's not the only way. Let's explore other paths. Let's try something new—Augmentative and Alternative Communication… AAC."

They looked hesitant, even disappointed at first. Their hope had been centered around hearing their son speak words aloud. I understood that. But I also knew that communication could bloom in other ways—through gestures, visuals, and devices. We started the intervention slowly. The first few sessions were tough—the child was restless, the parents unsure.

But then, something shifted.

The child began picking up skills, responding to pictures, using gestures, and calming down during sessions. Communication started making sense to him in a way speech hadn't so far. His meltdowns have reduced. He began pointing to what he wanted instead of crying. His parents watched in awe.

A few weeks later, they shared something that stayed with me. With a smile, they told me,
"We now understand how to manage speech problems and that there are alternate methods to help our child communicate".

This changed everything for me; that was a win.

Not just because of the progress the child made, but because the parents gained knowledge and hope they hadn't felt in years. As a speech-language pathologist, moments like this mean everything. Empowering families is, in fact, the first step toward progress. Therapy isn't just about teaching language—it's about creating connection, building trust, and opening a door where it once felt like there were only walls.

That day, the fear I used to carry in my pockets felt just a little lighter. I had helped a child communicate. I had helped a family understand.

And slowly, with each story like this, I was learning to find my voice too.

Part 3
LEARNING BEYOND BOOKS

Real growth doesn't just happen in classrooms or through textbooks. The most important lessons often come from experience, stepping into real situations, facing new challenges, and connecting with people whose lives are very different from your own. In this part, my story moves beyond lectures and written notes to the living, unpredictable lessons found in hospital corridors, therapy rooms, and the everyday moments of working and learning.

Here, "learning" means listening with empathy, adapting to new environments, and discovering wisdom in both mistakes and successes. It's about finding courage when things feel uncertain, asking questions that aren't in any syllabus, and learning more about yourself while helping others. Step into a world where knowledge grows with every interaction and where becoming a true professional means learning with both head and heart.

"Books give you answers, life gives you understanding."

8
The Power of Listening

Listening is more than just staying quiet while someone talks. It's about paying close attention, showing respect, and truly trying to understand what another person feels. In the beginning, I wasn't a great listener—but as a young speech therapist, I quickly learned that my job was not just about helping children speak. It was also about listening deeply: to the children, their families, and even to my doubts.

I soon realized that **listening is a real gift**. When people know you're truly hearing them, they feel respected, important, and less alone. For many parents of children with disabilities, this means a lot. Their journey is not easy, their struggles are often invisible, their mental health can suffer, and their parenting life is different from others. Sometimes, they aren't looking for solutions. They just want someone to listen to their feelings, their worries, and their hopes.

One thing I started doing in every session was a simple check-in,

I would pause for a moment before jumping into therapy, look at the parent, and ask, "How are you doing, sir/madam?" Just taking a few minutes to listen made a big difference. I could see parents relax, open up, and feel valued. These moments didn't solve every problem, but they made the parents feel heard and soulful. It reminded them and me that their well-being mattered too.

I always tell parents, "Only when you take care of yourself can you help your child be happy and learn." Your health is just as important as your child's. My role isn't only to help the child, but to support and listen to the parents as well.

Over time, I discovered that real change didn't come from having all the answers, but from listening closely with patience and an open heart. In learning this, I built stronger connections, grew in my work, and gained lessons no book could ever teach.

"The power of listening" isn't just about therapy—it's about kindness, understanding, and giving people the space to feel seen.

9
Mentor and Mistakes
The Sculptors of My Journey

From the very start, my life has been touched and shaped by wonderful mentors—teachers, professors, and guides. I have always felt deep respect and gratitude for them. Without their patient guidance, I wouldn't be where I am today. Mentors are like sculptors: gently carving away doubts, smoothing rough edges, and helping us discover our true shape. I am grateful for each one, from my earliest school days to my first steps as a speech therapist. Without their guidance, I would be just a stone—thank you, and thank you to God for blessing me with such incredible mentors.

A Lesson on a Busy Day

One hectic day early in my career, a parent and child came in for an assessment. The session flowed, but I noticed some answers came from the mother, not the child. After therapy, I filled in all the scores, feeling good about my work—until my seniors noticed something odd: the scores were unusually high. They mentioned this to my mentor.

Instead of scolding me, my mentor approached with quiet kindness. “What happened, Kevin? Why are your scores so high?” she asked. Her gentle voice made it easy to admit what had happened. Side by side, we sat down to review my mistake together. She explained that using a parent’s answers instead of the child’s can give a false idea of the child’s abilities. She taught me it’s better to wait, try again, and only score what you truly observe. If the child cannot or will not respond, simply note it as a parental report, don’t force a score, and don’t rush.

When she asked, “Do you understand, Kevin?” I felt safe enough to admit my error. She reassured me, “It’s okay, you’re learning. Mistakes are part of the process. As you gain experience, you’ll make fewer of them.”

What amazed me most was her response. She didn’t raise her voice or make me feel embarrassed. Her calmness and understanding turned a mistake into a valuable lesson:

- Mistakes are what teachers learn from.
- Always act with kindness, even when correcting others.

The Gift of Space and Trust

What set my mentor apart was the space she gave me to grow. She trusted me, almost as if she were my big sister and I was her little brother. While others sometimes felt closely monitored, my mentor gave me freedom to experiment, stumble, and pick myself up again.

When I hesitated or doubted myself, I'd ask, "Can I try this, ma'am?" Her answer was always the same: a warm smile and a simple, "Try it, Kevin. Go for it." Her belief in me made it easier to take chances, learn from failures, and celebrate my small victories. No idea was too silly, no mistake too big for her to lose faith in me. With her cheerful encouragement, I found the confidence I needed.

She was my backbone, ready to catch me if I fell, but never holding me back from trying. Her gentle guidance and unwavering support gave me the courage to become better each day.

What Mentors Teach

As a young therapist, I now see that mistakes are not the end, just new beginnings. Don't be afraid to get things wrong; talk to your mentors, ask questions, and make corrections. That's how real professionals grow.

Mentors care for us, guide us, and inspire us to do more. To all my mentors: thank you, from the bottom of my heart. You deserve all my gratitude; without you, I would not be the person I am today.

10
Lessons Never Known

Every patient who walked into my therapy room carried more than a case file and a diagnosis—they brought stories, emotions, and reflections of life that I had never seen from this angle before. There were victories I still carry in my heart—and there were painful moments I will never forget.

Some stories were filled with breakthroughs, patience, and growth. Others were harder—stalled progress despite relentless effort, unexpected setbacks, and sometimes, relationships that fractured under the weight of worry.

I met parents whose love could move mountains. They arrived exhausted, desperate for answers, yet willing to pour every drop of energy into helping their child grow. Their courage in the face of uncertainty taught me the purest form of resilience.

But I also encountered a different reality—one that left a distinct mark on me. Among some young parents, I began to notice patterns. Disagreements between husband and wife are slipping into therapy sessions. Miscommunication becomes rejection. One parent stayed silent while the other blamed. Sometimes, they couldn't even agree on what their child needed—because they hadn't yet figured out how to be partners, let alone parents.

Watching these moments repeat in small but piercing ways, I began to feel a quiet fear grow inside me—not of professional failure, but of something deeply personal: "marriage and relationships". I wondered, Is this what love becomes over time? Blame instead of teamwork, denial instead of acceptance?

A question lodged itself in my heart:
We teach sexual education in schools by the twelfth grade, understanding it's an important life skill. But "why don't we teach parenting skills?" Parenting is a lifelong responsibility, yet we leave people to figure it out with no preparation.

In my work, this gap becomes painfully clear—especially when I see "parents with low temperament skills". Temperament—the natural way a person thinks, feels, and behaves—is an inborn part of personality that influences our reactions to situations, people, and emotions. Parents who struggle to manage their emotions or to engage warmly often struggle with social interaction. And when this happens, conversations with their children become fewer, flatter, and less engaging. This is one of the **biggest missing pieces in child development**... and one we rarely talk about.

For many, parenting skills are inherited directly from their parents—whether good or bad. People who had a difficult, trauma-filled childhood often carry those wounds into adulthood without realizing it. When they don't know what positive, nurturing parenting looks like, they may lose hope in their partner, in family life, even in themselves. Too often, we end up learning parenting the hard way—through mistakes and trial and error—without the safety net of structured guidance.

In moments like this, I thought of my parents. They weren't perfect. They argued. They sometimes misunderstood each other. But above all, what lived in our home was not resentment but "love, endurance, and acceptance". They didn't always agree, but they always showed up—for each other, and me. That, I have learned, is the quiet magic that can keep a family alive.

Sitting in those therapy rooms, watching so many versions of parenthood, I slowly began to understand a truth that has stayed with me:
"Not all parenting is the same. Not all love feels safe. And not everyone is ready to raise a child when they have not yet learned how to raise each other".
But when it works—when parents stand united even in their struggles, when love survives disagreement, when acceptance overrides fear—it is nothing short of magic. And that kind of love is something worth believing in.

Some parents taught me how fragile relationships can be under pressure. Others reminded me that love, even imperfect, can still anchor a home. I learned from their lives—not just about how a child learns language, but how families, in their way, teach patience, empathy, and the courage to show up even when it's hard.

For me, the most important thing is this—"love is not about perfection, it's about accepting imperfections".

Through it all, I came to realize: I don't just work with children. I work with the echoes of homes, the strength of relationships, and the vulnerability of people learning to love through pain and pressure. And with every story, I learn not just how to be a better therapist... but how to be a better human being.

PART 4
FINDING MYSELF

Earlier in my story, I wrote a chapter called "Who Am I?", a question so many of us begin with as we start to understand ourselves. Back then, my thoughts were shaped by what others expected: doing well in school, aiming for a good college, and landing a respected job. Those were the standards set by my parents, neighbors, and society. Like many, I was guided by the voices around me, and my search for identity was often colored by their hopes and judgments.

But as life moved forward, I found that the answer to "Who am I?" wasn't fixed. Life comes in phases, and each brings its lessons, doubts, and discoveries. I passed through moments of happiness, failures, heartbreak, success, and loss. Every experience changed how I saw myself.

Now, moving from that early question, I am focusing on "finding myself," a journey that's less about others' expectations and more about listening to my own heart. This new phase is about understanding what truly matters to me, accepting my flaws and strengths, and having the courage to step into the unknown, even when doubts appear.

In these chapters, you'll see how I've grown from simply asking "Who am I?" to exploring and embracing who I am becoming. Each phase, from accepting myself to moving forward after setbacks, listening inward, showing courage, and growing through challenges, has helped shape my answer.

Finding myself isn't about reaching a final answer. It's about accepting that life changes and so do we. We continue to ask, learn, and grow with every new phase, and a new piece of the puzzle falls into place. And in sharing this journey, I hope to encourage others to do the same: to look inward with honesty, to embrace every phase, and to welcome the ever-changing adventure of truly finding yourself.

11
Half a promise

Some people enter your life so quietly that you don't even notice until everything has already begun to change. It all started during our clinical postings in college. She was just another teammate at first, someone I expected to work with for a few months. But even in those early days, something about her felt familiar. What began as routine conversations between patient visits slowly became longer chats, laughter, and shared worries about our future careers.

We began walking together after shifts, helping each other during stressful sessions, and finding joy in the little things like chai breaks, inside jokes, and quiet study evenings. Our friendship naturally deepened. Over time, we realized this wasn't just a friendship anymore. We were falling in love.

Of course, we had our doubts.

Will this work?
Can we manage two demanding careers?

Are we ready for what lies ahead?

We spoke about these fears openly. We prayed. We leaned on faith and supported each other through uncertainty. And eventually, we made a decision to give our relationship a real chance. For a while, it was one of the most beautiful chapters of my life. The kind of love that made even ordinary days feel special. People around us noticed. Our bond was strong, hopeful, and full of dreams.

But life had other plans.

One rainy evening, after a long day at the hospital, I was sitting alone in my tiny rented room. My phone rang. Her voice was soft, shaking a little.

“We’ll call it off, Kevin,” she said. “It’s over.”

I didn’t understand at first. I thought it was just a bad day or a misunderstanding. But it wasn’t. That single sentence shattered the future I had imagined with her. Everything we talked about working in different cities but staying close, cheering each other on, building something together, vanished in that moment.

I cried. I tried to convince her. I begged. But it was already over.

Lost and shattered, I called my mother. I didn’t know what to say, so I just cried. She didn’t ask questions. She listened. After a long pause, she simply said, “It’s okay, Kevin. This is life. It’s hard now, but you’ll be okay.”

Her words gave me just enough strength to breathe.

That night, I couldn't sleep. My heart felt too heavy. The walls around me felt tighter than usual. I had a good job, but no excitement to wake up. I had responsibilities, but no will. I was supposed to be building a new life, but the foundation had just crumbled.

Yet the next day, I showed up. To work. To life. To whatever was next.

What followed were some of the hardest weeks of my life. Some mornings, I didn't want to get out of bed. A song, a photo, a memory, everything reminded me of her. Some nights I stayed up hoping for a message. Her favorite dress, her voice in my memory, her last texts haunted me like echoes I didn't ask for.

But even in the middle of that pain, I couldn't blame her.

She had taught me what love truly was. She helped me grow in faith during our internship. We used to read a Bible chapter together before work. She brought out a spiritual side of me I hadn't known before. For that, I'll always be thankful.

People often say, "You'll get over it," as if it's a simple task. But the truth is, I didn't "get over" anything. I simply learned to live with it. I smiled at work. I acted normally with friends. I listened to others' problems, even as I was quietly drowning in my own.

Time didn't erase the pain—it only dulled its sharpness.

Even months later, the word “breakup” felt like a wound. It made me nervous about love, about trust, about letting anyone that close again. But I slowly realized: this was now part of my story.

Not a story of loss.
A story of becoming.

I learned that people who love you can still walk away. That even the best promises can be broken. But I also learned that even with a heavy heart, you can keep showing up. And that’s the bravest thing you can do.

I never stopped respecting her or what we had. I never let it turn into regret. And somewhere in all that pain, I found a new version of myself wiser, stronger, more grounded.

That was the day my heart changed.
Not because it broke,
But because it learned how to heal.

“Sometimes, the person who breaks your heart also opens your eyes”.

12
Lonely Nights, Big Questions

There was a time when I was never really alone.

In school, in college, even during my internship, life felt like it was lived in a crowd. My friends were always around. We'd eat together, laugh over the smallest things, and stay up late talking about everything from career goals to the most random YouTube videos. You didn't have to make plans; plans just happened. And if one person dropped a "let's go," five others followed. It was noisy, chaotic, and beautiful.

But life began to change quietly.

It didn't happen overnight. It started with one person getting a job in another city. Another got busy with higher studies. A few friends fell in love, and their worlds shifted. Slowly, our calls reduced. Our conversations turned into short replies. And before I realized it, the group that once filled every day with energy... became silent.

When I moved to Vellore, I was full of excitement. It felt like everything I had worked for was finally falling into place: my first job, my first step into the real world, and the start of the career I had always dreamed about. But once the busy hospital shifts ended and I returned to my little rented room, a quiet feeling would settle in. I should've felt complete... but deep down, something felt missing.

It was a Sunday. I had no duties, no pending work. I walked to a nearby restaurant and took a corner seat. I looked around—families laughing, college groups sharing fries, couples in quiet conversation. And then there was me, just... sitting there, pretending to scroll through my phone. That was the first time I felt alone.

At first, the silence was loud.

I missed being called randomly just to share memes. I missed group rides, late-night food runs, and the comfort of knowing someone was always a message away. I started noticing how long it had been since I heard "Where are you? Let's meet."

But over time, something shifted.

The quiet started teaching me things that the crowd never could. I began doing things I never thought I'd do alone, walking to the church in the evening, reading a book in a cafe, spending hours just sitting on the hospital bench after duty, watching the sky change.

And in those still moments, questions began to rise:

What do I enjoy doing?

What does success mean to me, not what others think it should be?

Who am I when no one is watching, when there's no one to impress?

I didn't have all the answers. I still don't. But slowly, I stopped trying to escape the silence. I started listening to it. I realized that maybe this phase of loneliness wasn't punishment—it was preparation. It was the world slowing me down, so I could meet myself properly.

I still miss my old days, my friends, and the boy who never had to think twice about companionship. But now I understand something deeper: growing up isn't just about getting a degree or a job. It's about learning to stand alone sometimes—and be okay with it.

And the best part? I know now that when I reconnect with my friends—whenever that may be—I'll have stories to tell that were written in quiet, not just in chaos.

"Loneliness isn't the absence of people, it's the presence of growth waiting to happen."

13
Small wins, quite purpose

Some days just begin quietly with a walk to work, a half-sleepy breakfast, and the same hospital hallway you've walked a hundred times before. Nothing new. Nothing loud.

That morning, I didn't do anything extraordinary. I finished my session notes without triple-checking every word. It may not sound like much, but for me, it was a first. No second-guessing. No anxiety. Just trust in what I have done.

Later that day, I noticed a mother sitting outside the therapy room, her eyes heavy with questions she didn't know how to ask. I didn't have all the answers, but I sat beside her for a minute and simply said,
"You're doing your best."
She smiled, not the wide kind, but the soft, tired kind that says, "Thank you for seeing me."

No one clapped. No one noticed. But I did. And that night, I slept well—not because something big happened, but because something quiet settled in me. A little peace. A little pride.

A few months ago, I wouldn't have believed this would be enough.

Back then, I was always trying to prove something. I'd over-talk in meetings, afraid to seem invisible. I'd rehearse every sentence in my head before speaking. I was terrified of leading a session alone. But somehow, slowly, I started to trust myself.

I still remember a turning point. I was sent to attend a conference in Dharwad, a place I'd never even heard of. After the last session, I reached the train station hours early for my night train back to Bangalore. No Wi-Fi. No noise. Just me, on a bench, watching life move around me.

I saw families rushing with luggage, vendors shouting, and trains coming and going. But I sat still.
For the first time in a while, I wasn't in a hurry. I wasn't anxious. I just... was.

And in that silence, I thought about how far I'd come. From being a boy always surrounded by friends to someone traveling alone, working in a new city, and learning to connect with children in Hindi, Bangla, and Malayalam. There were no big milestones—just small steps. But they added up.

Now, when someone asks me what growth looks like, I don't talk about promotions or praise. I think of that quiet bench. That soft smile. That nod from a senior colleague in the hallway.

Because sometimes, the most important shifts happen on the most ordinary days.

So if you're waiting for a big moment to feel proud—don't. Just look at your small wins. Notice them. Feel them. Because real purpose lives in those little moments that pass by quietly, but change you forever.

"Small step makes big moves"

14
Friendships, Failures, First Salary

When I first moved to Vellore for work, everything felt unfamiliar. The first days were awkward, surrounded by colleagues who seemed distant and faces I couldn't yet read. But surprisingly, those strangers didn't stay strangers for long. Soon, colleagues turned into friends, and playing football introduced me to people from other departments. The same folks I once felt nervous around gradually became my chosen family away from home.

We made memories everywhere: late-night hangouts, movie outings, countless tea breaks, and trying food at every spot around the city. Some friendships became deeper than I ever expected, while others drifted apart, teaching me about trust, forgiveness, and letting go. Even now, I keep in touch with a few close college friends through our twice-weekly calls. There's one friend who's been with me since college began, standing by me in every moment, believing in me even when I doubted myself. She's a constant encourager, a guiding light, no matter the distance between us.

During my time in Vellore, two people meant the world to me. One was always there in silence, guiding me spiritually with prayers, songs, and faith, a reminder of how important it is to stay close to God. His ideas and relationship with God inspired me and helped me grow.

The other, she pulled me forward with her energy and care. In moments when loneliness crept in, she checked on me, asked how I was, listened to my worries, and stood by me during tough times. Her words pushed me to think wisely, and she never hesitated to support me, even when conflict arose at work. Late-night talks, small breaks, shared jokes, all of it made me feel like I belonged. They weren't just there for fun; they became the support system I never knew I needed.

If you're lucky enough to find friends like these, cherish them. In this world, true friends are rare. And friendship is sacred, don't take it for granted, and don't expect anything in return. A real friend helps without conditions.

Then came a milestone I'll never forget: my first job, and with it, my very first salary. The excitement was real. I remember that rush when my phone buzzed: *Your A/C xxxxxx5068 has been credited with a salary of Rs*****.

As a middle-class boy, that amount felt huge. I was overjoyed and called my parents right away—their happiness was bigger than any prize. With that first paycheck, I bought a new mobile phone for my mom, a promise I'd always wanted to keep. Being able to give something back to my family was a feeling beyond words.

Looking back, those early days full of new beginnings, strong friendships, hard lessons, and the pride of my first salary—remind me that every stage of life brings its meaning. Some moments break you, others build you. But in the end, it's the simple acts of caring and the bonds you cherish that matter most, making every step of the journey worth it.

Part 5
THAT ONE YEAR

I didn't know it at the time, but I was walking into a year that would quietly change everything.

It wasn't always loud or dramatic. There were no fireworks, no big announcements. Just a 21-year-old boy with a packed bag, stepping into a new city, a new job, and a life that felt too big to understand.

Some days were full of laughter, others full of questions. Some nights I stayed up dreaming, other nights I just stared at the ceiling, wondering what I was doing. I met people who became lessons, faced fears I never expected, and found strength in the smallest wins.

Looking back, that one year didn't just pass by; it left a mark. A soft but steady reminder that growth isn't always loud, but it is always real.

So, if you've ever felt lost, lonely, excited, confused, hopeful, all in the same week, this part is for you.

15
Heartfelt

Sometimes, all it takes is a pause to realize just how much life has changed.

One full moon night, there was a gentle breeze as I sat on my terrace, enjoying a warm cup of hot chocolate. I looked up at the bright moon, feeling the peace of the quiet night. In that moment, a question rose in my mind: “What have you earned all these days, Kevin?”

My thoughts drifted back over the years. Life had surprised me with unexpected turns, the decisions I had made, the people I lost, the places I had to leave behind, and the struggles that tested me. I recalled the silent strength I found living alone, facing new responsibilities, and meeting new people in strange places. I remembered friendships that blossomed when I needed them most and memories that became part of who I am.

Thinking about it, I answered myself honestly. I have gained good people, wonderful memories, new skills, and above all, a closer relationship with God. I realized in that moment just how blessed I have been. Grateful simply isn't a big enough word.

Gratitude, for me, is not only about the good things. It's also about the tough moments, the lessons learned, the small victories, and the quiet resilience that grew inside me. I still remember the early days, eyes full of tears, unsure if I could manage on my own, missing home and family. But now, when tears come, they're not for worry, but for pride that I made it through, that I didn't give up.

As a young professional, I started by assisting my seniors, listening, learning, and taking every piece of advice to heart. Now, I find myself working independently, making decisions with confidence, and seeing life through a wiser, kinder lens.

Every single moment, good or bad, has helped shape who I am. Every obstacle has added a little more strength and wisdom. Looking back today, I see not just the struggles but the courage it took to move through them. And for that, I am truly grateful.

Grateful for the journey.
Grateful for the people who walked beside me.
Grateful for the growth, the lessons, the memories.
And most of all, grateful to God for turning even uncertain days into something meaningful.

That night, under the gentle glow of the moon, I realized that even in the quietest moments, there is so much to be thankful for.

16
Irreversible

We all encounter moments in life that send us down unexpected paths. Often, we don't know if these turns are for better or worse, but we hold onto hope that they'll lead us somewhere meaningful. For me, entering Christian Medical College (CMC) was exactly such a turning point, a new trajectory for my career and life that I never planned.

CMC touched every part of who I am, from their unwavering ethics and belief in God to the way people there cared for one another. I witnessed how they treated patients with justice, respected juniors, and above all, saw every colleague not just as a professional, but as a human being.

What truly touched my heart was something simple but powerful: whenever I was worried or stressed, my colleagues and friends would pause and ask, "Can I pray for you?" In today's busy world, so few take time to bring their needs to God, but at CMC, everything began with prayer, every week and every journey guided by faith.

This meant a great deal to me. I grew up in a Christian community, close to God through childhood—until school and life took over, and my connection faded. During my undergraduate years, Sundays and prayers grew rare. Yet at CMC, I found my way back—attending prayers, joining fellowships, even sharing God's word myself.

I came to treasure the Bible verse Micah 6:8: "He has shown you, O mortal, what is good. And what does the LORD require of you? To act justly and to love mercy and to walk humbly with your God."

These words taught me to do what is right, show love as God does, and remain humble, no matter what I achieve. They changed my outlook and my life, reminding me that being a true follower of Christ is more than a label—it's a daily commitment.

But the changes at CMC were not just spiritual. Professionally, I found growth I'd never dreamed possible. I was once the boy who sat at the back, unnoticed now, but I was invited as a guest speaker at an autism program, welcomed and honored at the very front.

This wasn't just my doing, but the result of the team and the nurturing environment CMC provided. The transformation was so profound and lasting, it became a part of me, a change that can't be undone.

Sometimes, a place becomes more than just a location; it becomes the chapter that changes your entire story. CMC turned overwhelming days into a second home. Strangers became friends, friends became family, and the biggest challenges became the moments I learned to care, to persevere, and to believe in myself and others.

At CMC, I discovered a deeper sense of purpose, a calling for service, humility, and compassion. The community, the faith, the support, and the lessons will stay with me for a lifetime. That's why, for me, CMC changed me forever.

17

The Road Ahead – Dreams for the Future

The road ahead is full of promise and possibility. After all the lessons learned, the challenges overcome, and the growth experienced, I find myself standing at a new beginning—ready to dream bigger and reach higher.

Looking forward, I see not just a career path, but a life filled with purpose. My experiences at CMC and beyond have taught me the value of perseverance, compassion, and faith. These are the pillars on which I will build my future.

I dream of impacting lives—not just through my profession but with kindness and understanding. I want to keep growing, learning, and becoming a better version of myself every day. Challenges will come, but now I face them with confidence, knowing that every step forward matters. More than anything, I want to live meaningfully. To be present for the people I love, to contribute to my community, and to keep walking humbly with God. My journey has only just begun, and the road ahead is wide open.

With hope in my heart and faith as my guide, I step into tomorrow—ready to embrace whatever comes, knowing that dreams are not just wishes but the blueprints of our future.

As I began planning to pursue my master's abroad, I threw myself into IELTS preparation. Every test, every late night, and each small victory felt monumental. My parents went above and beyond, arranging a loan to support my education, and I engaged a consultant to help me navigate the complex admissions process.

Still, anxiety gnawed at me. Where should I go? Which country? The "cheapest" path still costs 40 lakhs—an unimaginable amount. The loan weighed on me, with an 8.5% interest rate, plus the added expenses of living far from home. I told myself I'd come back—serve my community, not settle abroad. But the worry was relentless: how could I shoulder this debt and not be a burden on those I love?

Nights blurred into days. I couldn't sleep. My mind spun with dreams and doubts. Was this life really for me? Did I have to choose between my hopes and my family?

Even the simplest things became hard. Eating. Smiling. Facing friends whose own journeys seemed dazzling and effortless. Peer pressure loomed: "If they can, why can't you?" But inside, a quieter voice reminded me that my path, and my responsibilities, might demand something different.

If I grow here, my whole community grows—not just my family.

One evening, heart pounding, I approached my Head of Department for a letter of recommendation. “Why do you want to go abroad? How much is the fee?” he asked. When I told him—40 lakhs—he looked shocked. “I’m not giving you a letter to waste 40 lakhs,” he replied. In that moment, I felt the world pause. Was this the sign I needed?

Confused, I called my professor for advice. I called my parents. “It’s your wish,” they said. The responsibility was mine alone.

And so, with a million thoughts and one heart full of both dreams and doubts, I stood quietly—not with a definite answer, but with a quiet resolve to listen—not to the noise around me, but to the still voice within.

I closed my laptop—the admission offer glowing on the screen. I turned off my phone—visa updates and flight messages fading into silence. I sat on the terrace, under a sky thick with stars and questions. For the first time in weeks, I breathed without a sense of pressure.

Maybe I’ll fly.
Maybe I’ll stay.
Maybe there’s something entirely unexpected just around the corner.

Did I chase the dream I’d clung to for so long—or find a new one, quietly blooming where I least expected?
All I know is, the journey isn’t over. Not even close.

“The story is just beginning.”

To be continued...

9 788199 325074

Printed at Repro India Ltd.